# For my family,
# the whole lot of you!

First edition

First published in Great Britain in 2020 by Robyn Wrenny
First published in paperback in 2020

Text © Robyn Wrenny
Illustrations © Robyn Wrenny

Print ISBN: 9798575204053

www.robynwrenny.co.uk

# The Fox and the Acorn

In far away lands, in a forest of old,

where the trees and the ground were eternally cold,

where the snow never melted, and the wind bit and howled,

there all was sadness, and there Winter prowled.

No greenery grew, no flowers to see,

and for the poor frozen critters, there was little to eat.

But there in the snow there was one golden heart,

who made warmth and compassion and helping an art.

Digging for those who were little and weak,
she uncovered rich roots for the
poor and the meek.

The white Winter fox, beloved by all.
Known to come to the aid
of any who called.

And one who called "help!", was her snowy owl friend,

who had a freshly made nest and new eggs to tend.

"Snow and ice all around, but it is warmth that they need!"

The poor owl was stuck with naught but a plea.

"Take some of my fur,

I have quite a lot."

Said generous, sweet creature

Winter the Fox.


"And worry not Owl,

I have plenty to spare.

May your babies hatch strong,

lovely and fair."

And the grateful owl, her eggs warm and nestled,

produced something small, and smooth like a pebble.

She fluttered down from her perch and onto the snow,

with the pebble to beak, and lifted to show...

Not a pebble at all, but something precious and dear.

One tiny gold acorn, Winter saw as she neared.

Owl hooted her thanks for the generous aid,

and gave her very last acorn by way of a trade.

Then a memory stirred, only faintly at first,

Of the story of how their
poor forest was cursed.

It told of a dragon, huge
and heavy with greed,

Who stole the land's riches,
a horrid misdeed.

He took all there was, every treasure in sight,

until snow came to fall, cold and pale in the night.

Spring would never return, and nothing would grow.

All of the animals trapped in a cold winter woe.

But maybe this dragon she could journey to meet.
Because no treasure was rarer, no gold could compete.

Perhaps, for the acorn,
        he would set them all free.

Would he banish this snow
    for his very own tree?

Winter looked to the mountains, distant they were,

whilst a chilling cold breeze came and ruffled her fur.

In the highest grey peak gleamed a spot like a star,

flickering orange and dreadfully far.

She made up her mind, decidedly so,

to test the truth in the rumours of that tiny warm glow.

A cave, so they said, where the dragon still slept,

on a pile of gold and the riches he kept.

Winter picked up the acorn and thought out a plot,

for the journey she started at a keen little trot.


She hurried along, until she came to a place

where the forest gave way to a wide treeless space.

A lake long since frozen, once deep, rich and blue,

now lay icy and still with deep cracks running through.

It creaked under paw, forcing Winter to slow.

Would it break? She wondered, with no way to know.

She tip-toed across, as only a fox can,

until there came a great crack, then oh how she ran!

And she didn't stop running until she was clear

of the great frozen lake, where she swallowed her fear.

The climb was the hardest, the snow rest so deep

that at times Winter moved at barely a creep.

There were boulders to jump, and huge cliffs to scale,

but Winter refused absolutely to fail.

Then just for a moment Winter came to a stop,

as the ground under foot turned to granite and rock.


She turned back from up high to look at the view,

and could see the whole forest, where nothing new grew.

Her little heart broke to see her home so forlorn.

But it was hers, she belonged there, it was where she was born.

So save it she would! Her strength was renewed.

She only hoped that the dragon was in a good mood.

She continued her climb, but had barely begun

when she found the cave mouth, shining bright like the sun.

She could feel the heat as it tickled her nose,

and felt soothing and warm on her poor tired toes.

Winter dug deep for her courage, held onto it tight,

and walked into the cave to a breath taking sight...

...A cavern enormous, all glittering gold,

with piles and piles of riches of old.

Gemstones and jewels, chalices, crowns,

but from under the hoard came a frightening sound;

Great rumbling snores, each one billowing smoke.

Then as though he had sensed her the great dragon awoke.

He stretched and he yawned,
scattering gold all around.

Great angry eyes opened,
and then Winter they found.

He growled as he loomed,
glittering scales so fine.

"Who dares enter my cave?
These riches are MINE!"

Winter looked up in awe,
amazed by his might,
Where any other critter
would have taken a fright.

She put down the acorn
on a plate made of gold,
and stood up to the dragon,
little but bold.

"Our forest is frozen, they say you are to blame –

When your greed brought you here and you stated your claim.

But you trade wishes for riches, or so it is told.

So please, take this acorn, save our home from this cold!"

The Dragon laughed a deep laugh,
smoky and mean.

"You must be the most foolhardy
fox I have seen.

One worthless acorn
is not nearly enough.

Now get out!" He snarled,
impatient and gruff.

Winter fluffed in offense
at his horrible greed,
To laugh and dismiss
all of the creatures in need.

"You are foolish to miss
the potential it holds.
The last tree would be worth
more than all of your gold!"

At first, he said nothing but growled and rumbled,

As the brave little fox had him quiet and humbled.

"The last tree?" He wondered, voice low
and gritty,

And he felt, for the first time,
a great swell of pity.

The dragon was moved,
he had been awfully cruel.

For one acorn was greater
than the greatest of jewels.

Without a word more
he snatched it away,

and heaved himself out
into the cold light of day.

His breath looked like clouds
in the cool winter air,
as he lumbered over the earth,
rocky,
empty
and bare.

He raked a deep trench with dragonish ease,
dropped the acorn within, and breathed
a warm breeze.

And then...

And then, just like magic,
the acorn started to sprout.
A tiny green leaf began
to work its way out.

From that one little leaf,
Spring started to spread.
And Winter herself, well...

...she began to turn red!

Colour returned,
flowing over the land.

The trees found their leaves,
the forest turned grand.

The frozen lake thawed,
and started to flow,

and the stormy clouds
parted to let the sun show.

The drake watched the sapling
for one moment more,

"I will keep it in good health."
To the red fox he swore.

"The snow will not ravage
these lands from today.

When the next winter comes,
I will not let it stay."

Then gone was the drake,
back to his cavern to sleep.
Winter gave thanks to his tail,
fading into the keep.

So she set off for home,
and ran the whole way.
Stopping but once at the lake,
to paddle and play.

The forest thrived after.
Every critter did well.

The seasons were fair,
thanks to the great dragon's spell.

And when snow fell too hard, or lasted too long...
The dragon breathed it away,
so that his tree could grow strong.

Printed in Poland
by Amazon Fulfillment
Poland Sp. z o.o., Wrocław

66225471R00026